Iris and Walter
The School Play

Iris and Walter
The School Play

WRITTEN BY

Elissa Haden Guest

ILLUSTRATED BY

Christine Davenier

GULLIVER BOOKS

HARCOURT, INC.

SAN DIEGO   NEW YORK   LONDON

For my best friend, Jenny—E. H. G.

For Liz and Lily—C. D.

Text copyright © 2003 by Elissa Haden Guest
Illustrations copyright © 2003 by Christine Davenier

www.HarcourtBooks.com

Gulliver Books is a trademark of Harcourt, Inc.,
registered in the United States of America and/or other jurisdictions.

Library of Congress Cataloging-in-Publication Data
Guest, Elissa Haden.
Iris and Walter: the school play/written by Elissa Haden Guest;
illustrated by Christine Davenier.
p. cm.— (Iris and Walter; 5)
"Gulliver Books."
Summary: Iris is devastated when she has to miss being in her first
school play because she is sick.
[1. Theater—Fiction. 2. Schools—Fiction. 3. Sick—Fiction.]
I. Title: School play. II. Davenier, Christine, ill. III. Title.
PZ7.G9375Isr 2003
[E]—dc21 2002006373
ISBN 0-15-216481-2

First edition
H G F E D C B A
Printed in Singapore

Contents

1. Exciting News

Iris and her best friend, Walter,
raced outside after school.
They had exciting news to tell Grandpa.
"Our class is putting on a play!" said Iris.
"What's the play about?" asked Grandpa.
"It's about bugs," said Iris.

"I'm going to be a dragonfly," said Walter.
"And I'm going to be a cricket," said Iris.
"I have three lines to say,
and Walter has three lines, too!"

"And Miss Cherry said that
after the play we're going to have
an ice-cream party," said Walter.
"What fun!" said Grandpa.

That evening, Iris told her parents
and Baby Rose all about the play.
"Do you want to hear my lines?" she asked.
"Of course," said her mother.
"I can't wait," said her father.
"Quiet, everyone," said Grandpa.

Iris opened her notebook and read:
"I am a cricket. I chirp and hop.
My ears are on my front legs."
"Ears on your legs!" said Iris's mother.
"Well, how about that," said Iris's father.
"You'll make a wonderful cricket,"
said Grandpa.

Iris said her lines at dinner.

She said her lines to Baby Rose.

And by the time Iris fell asleep,
she knew all her lines by heart.

2. Stage Fright

The next day, Miss Cherry said,
"This morning you are all
going to work on your costumes."
"Oh good," said Walter.
Walter loved to paint and draw.
"And while you are working,
you can practice your lines,"
said Miss Cherry.
"Great," said Iris.
Iris loved saying her lines.

"Will you help me with my lines, Iris?"
asked Walter.
"Sure," said Iris.
"Will you help me paint my wings?"
"Of course," said Walter.

Walter helped Iris with her wings.
They sparkled in the sunlight.
Iris helped Walter with his lines
until he knew them perfectly.

All week long, the children
practiced their lines.
The day before the play,
Miss Cherry said,
"Today we're having our dress rehearsal
on the school stage."

"I've never been
on a stage before," said Walter.
"Isn't it exciting?" said Iris.
"Remember to speak
your lines slowly," said Miss Cherry.
"And use a strong, loud voice.
You can go first, Walter."
"Okay," said Walter.

Walter cleared his throat.
"I...," said Walter.
But suddenly, Walter
could not remember his lines.

"I am a dragonfly," whispered Iris.
"I have four wings and six legs.
I eat mosquitoes."
"I am a dragonfly," said Walter.
"I have four wings and six legs.
I eat mosquitoes."

"Good," said Miss Cherry.
"You just need to practice
a little more, Walter.
I know you are going to do very well."

But now, Walter was worried.
"What if I forget my lines
when we do the play?"
he whispered to Iris.
"Don't worry," said Iris.
"*I* know your lines.
I can whisper them to you."
But Walter was still worried.

3. A Terrible Day

That night, Iris put on her costume
for Baby Rose and danced
around their room.
"You're coming to the play tomorrow, Rosie!"
Iris told her sister.

Baby Rose smiled and said, "Da, Da, Da."
"But you'll have to be very quiet, Rosie,"
said Iris. "You can't make any noise, okay?"

"Iris, my girl, what are you doing up?"
asked Grandpa.
"I'm not sleepy," said Iris. "I can't wait for
tomorrow."
"Even crickets need their sleep,"
said Grandpa. "Now close your eyes,
and before you know it, it will be morning."

The next day, Iris woke up very early.
Her head hurt.
Her throat was sore.
Iris was sick!

"Iris, my love," said Iris's mother,
"you have to stay in bed today."
"But today is the play!" croaked Iris.

"I know, my Iris," said Iris's father.
"But you can't go to school
when you have a fever."
"I can't miss the play," wailed Iris.
"I can't miss the ice-cream party.
And I have to help Walter
remember his lines!"

But Iris's parents would not
let her go to school.

They tucked her into their bed.
They brought her tea with honey.
They gave her blackberry candies
to soothe her throat.
Iris cried and cried.
After a while, she fell asleep.

Iris slept all day.
When she woke up, it was evening.
School was over.
There was a card on the table.

Dear Iris,
I remembered all my lines.
Get well soon.
Your best friend,
Walter

4. Better Days

On Monday,
Iris was well enough to go to school.
"Look, everybody, Iris is back!" said Walter.
Iris felt as if she'd been gone a long time.
"Welcome back," said Miss Cherry.

"It's too bad you had
to miss the play," said Benny.
"Everyone clapped a lot,"
said Jenny.
"The ice-cream party was
so much fun!" said Lulu.

Iris felt a lump in her throat.
Her nose stung.

"Don't feel sad, Iris," said Walter.
"I missed the play," said Iris.
"I missed the ice-cream party.
I missed everything."

"I know it's hard," said Miss Cherry.
"But there will be other plays, Iris,
I promise."
"Later on, I'll have a surprise for
everyone," Miss Cherry whispered.
"I think you'll enjoy it."

At snack time, Miss Cherry said,
"Iris, will you help me pass out the surprise?"
When Iris saw the surprise,
she started to laugh.
There were green-frosted dragonfly cookies
and orange-and-yellow butterfly cookies.
There were cricket and ant
and ladybug cookies.

"How do you like my bug cookies?"
asked Miss Cherry.
"They're beautiful," said Benny.
"They're delicious," said Iris.
"I'm glad," said Miss Cherry.
"Now I'll tell you what
we are going to study next."

On the way home from school,
Iris and Walter had exciting news
to tell Grandpa.
"Our class is going to
put on a dance!" said Iris.

"It's about the solar system," said Walter.
"I'm going to be Mars."
"And I'm going to be the Sun," said Iris.
"You'll both be splendid," said Grandpa.
And they were.

The illustrations in this book were created in pen and ink on keacolor paper.
The display type was set in Elroy.
The text type was set in Fairfield Medium.
Color separations by Classic Scan Pte. Ltd., Singapore
Printed and bound by Tien Wah Press, Singapore
This book was printed on totally chlorine-free Enso Stora Matte paper.
Production supervision by Sandra Grebenar and Wendi Taylor
Designed by Lydia D'moch and Suzanne Fridley